Bart's Go-Cart

Level 3F

Written by Deborah Chancellor
Illustrated by Garyfalia Leftheri
Reading Consultant: Betty Franchi

About Phonics

Spoken English uses more than 40 speech sounds. Each sound is called a *phoneme*. Some phonemes relate to a single letter (d-o-g) and others to combinations of letters (sh-ar-p). When a phoneme is written down, it is called a *grapheme*. Teaching these sounds, matching them to their written form, and sounding out words for reading is the basis of phonics.

Early phonics instruction gives children the tools to sound out, blend, and say the words without having to rely on memory or guesswork. This instruction gives children the confidence and ability to read unfamiliar words, helping them progress toward independent reading.

About the Consultant

Betty Franchi is an American educator with a Bachelor's Degree in Elementary and Middle Education as well as a Master's Degree in Special Education. Betty holds a National Boards for Professional Teaching Standards certification. Throughout her 24 years as a teacher, she has studied and developed an expertise in Phonetic Awareness and has implemented phonetic strategies, teaching many young children to read, including students with special needs.

Reading tips

This book focuses on the *ar* sound as in park.

Tricky and/or new words in this book

Any words in bold may have unusual spellings or are new and have not yet been introduced.

> **Tricky and/or new words in this book**
>
> **the he for was look
> after liked to go**

Extra ways to have fun with this book

After the readers have finished the story, ask them questions about what they have just read.

What are the names of the boys in the story?
What happened when it got dark?

Explain that the two letters *ar* make one sound. Think of other words that make the *ar* sound, such as *bark* and *lark*.

I love racing in Bart's shiny new go-cart. It's really fast!

A Pronunciation Guide

This grid highlights the sounds used in the story and offers a guide on how to say them.

s as in sat	a as in ant	t as in tin	p as in pig	i as in ink
n as in net	c as in cat	e as in egg	h as in hen	r as in rat
m as in mug	d as in dog	g as in get	o as in ox	u as in up
l as in log	f as in fan	b as in bag	j as in jug	v as in van
w as in wet	z as in zip	y as in yet	k as in kit	qu as in quick
x as in box	ff as in off	ll as in ball	ss as in kiss	zz as in buzz
ck as in duck	pp as in puppy	nn as in bunny	rr as in arrow	gg as in egg
dd as in daddy	bb as in chubby	tt as in attic	sh as in shop	ch as in chip
th as in them	th as in the	ng as in sing	nk as in sunk	le as in bottle
ai as in rain	ee as in feet	ie as in pies	oa as in oak	ue as in cue
ar as in park				

Be careful not to add an /uh/ sound to /s/, /t/, /p/, /c/, /h/, /r/, /m/, /d/, /g/, /l/, /f/ and /b/. For example, say /ff/ not /fuh/ and /sss/ not /suh/.

Mark went **to the** park.
He met Bart at the park.

Bart had a blue **go**-cart.

"**Look** at my new go-cart!"
said Bart.

"It is art."

Mark **liked** Bart's jazzy go-cart.
"Can I try?"

Mark went **for** a ride on Bart's go-cart in the park. He went quickly. He went fast. Zoom!

Bart was angry and argued
with Mark.

Bart tried to get Mark to stop.

"I want my go-cart back!"
he yelled.

It **was** very hard for Mark to stop and get off the go-cart.

"Can't stop me yet!"
Mark told Bart.

Bart ran **after** Mark
around the park.

It got dark.

Mark crashed the go-cart
into an oak tree.

"I can see stars," said Mark,
but he was not in pain.

Bart started to chuckle. "Never ride a go-cart in the dark!" he said.

"I'm sorry," said Mark.
"I still think it was a good night."

OVER 48 TITLES IN SIX LEVELS
Betty Franchi recommends...

Some titles from Level 1

I love reading phonics — **Bad Rat**
978 1 84898 747 0

I love reading phonics — **The Best Gift**
978 1 84898 750 0

I love reading phonics — **Clint and Grant Play I-Spy**
978 1 84898 752 4

I love reading phonics — **Bret and Grandma's Trip!**
978 1 84898 751 7

Some titles from Level 2

I love reading phonics — **Wish Fish**
978 1 84898 755 5

I love reading phonics — **Chuck and Duck**
978 1 84898 756 2

I love reading phonics — **Pink Bunny**
978 1 84898 760 9

I love reading phonics — **Let's go to the Swings**
978 1 84898 759 3

Other titles to enjoy from Level 3

I love reading phonics — **GOAT IN A BOAT**
978 1 84898 766 1

I love reading phonics — **Queen Ella's Feet**
978 1 84898 764 7

I love reading phonics — **Puff Flies**
978 1 84898 765 4

An Hachette Company
First Published in the United States by TickTock, an imprint of Octopus Publishing Group.
www.octopusbooksusa.com

Copyright © Octopus Publishing Group Ltd 2013

Distributed in the US by
Hachette Book Group USA
237 Park Avenue, New York NY 10017, USA

Distributed in Canada by
Canadian Manda Group
165 Dufferin Street, Toronto, Ontario, Canada M6K 3H6

ISBN 978 1 84898 768 5

Printed and bound in China
10 9 8 7 6 5 4 3 2 1